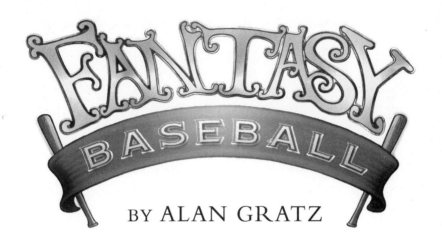

FANTASY BASEBALL

BY ALAN GRATZ

DIAL BOOKS FOR YOUNG READERS

an imprint of Penguin Group (USA) Inc.

DIAL BOOKS FOR YOUNG READERS
A division of Penguin Young Readers Group
Published by The Penguin Group
Penguin Group (USA) Inc., 375 Hudson Street,
New York, NY 10014, U.S.A.
Penguin Group (Canada), 90 Eglinton Avenue East,
Suite 700, Toronto, Ontario, Canada M4P 2Y3
(a division of Pearson Penguin Canada Inc.)
Penguin Books Ltd, 80 Strand, London WC2R 0RL, England
Penguin Ireland, 25 St. Stephen's Green, Dublin 2, Ireland
(a division of Penguin Books Ltd)
Penguin Group (Australia), 250 Camberwell Road, Camberwell, Victoria 3124, Australia (a division of
Pearson Australia Group Pty Ltd)
Penguin Books India Pvt Ltd, 11 Community Centre,
Panchsheel Park, New Delhi - 110 017, India
Penguin Group (NZ), 67 Apollo Drive, Rosedale, North Shore 0632,
New Zealand (a division of Pearson New Zealand Ltd)
Penguin Books (South Africa) (Pty) Ltd, 24 Sturdee Avenue,
Rosebank, Johannesburg 2196, South Africa
Penguin Books Ltd, Registered Offices:
80 Strand, London WC2R 0RL, England

The publisher does not have any control over and does not
assume any responsibility for author or third-party websites or their content.

Book design by Jasmin Rubero
Text set in Bembo
Printed in the U.S.A.

1 3 5 7 9 10 8 6 4 2

Library of Congress Cataloging-in-Publication Data
Gratz, Alan, date.
Fantasy baseball / by Alan Gratz.
p.   cm.
Summary: A twelve-year-old boy wakes up in Ever After, where he is recruited
by Dorothy to play first base for the Oz Cyclones in the
Ever After Baseball Tournament.
ISBN 978-0-8037-3463-0 (hardcover)
[1. Baseball—Fiction. 2. Characters in literature—Fiction.] I. Title.
PZ7.G77224Fan 2011
[Fic]—dc22
2010008126